W9-BCD-667

The Boxcar Children® Mysteries

The Boxcar Children
Surprise Island
The Yellow House Mystery
Mystery Ranch
Mike's Mystery
Blue Bay Mystery
The Woodshed Mystery
The Lighthouse Mystery
Mountain Top Mystery
Schoolhouse Mystery
Caboose Mystery
Houseboat Mystery
Snowbound Mystery
Tree House Mystery
Bicycle Mystery
Mystery in the Sand
Mystery Behind the Wall
Bus Station Mystery
Benny Uncovers a Mystery
The Haunted Cabin Mystery
The Deserted Library Mystery
The Animal Shelter Mystery
The Old Motel Mystery
The Mystery of the Hidden Painting
The Amusement Park Mystery
The Mystery of the Mixed-Up Zoo
The Camp Out Mystery
The Mystery Girl
The Mystery Cruise

The Disappearing Friend Mystery
The Mystery of the Singing Ghost
The Mystery in the Snow
The Pizza Mystery
The Mystery Horse
The Mystery at the Dog Show
The Castle Mystery
The Mystery on Ice
The Mystery of the Lost Village
The Mystery of the Purple Pool
The Ghost Ship Mystery
The Mystery in Washington DC
The Canoe Trip Mystery
The Mystery of the Hidden Beach
The Mystery of the Missing Cat
The Mystery at Snowflake Inn
The Mystery on Stage
The Dinosaur Mystery
The Mystery of the Stolen Music
The Mystery at the Ballpark
The Chocolate Sundae Mystery
The Mystery of the Hot Air Balloon
The Mystery Bookstore
The Pilgrim Village Mystery
The Mystery of the Stolen Boxcar
Mystery in the Cave
The Mystery on the Train
The Mystery at the Fair
The Mystery of the Lost Mine

THE DINOSAUR MYSTERY

created by
GERTRUDE CHANDLER WARNER

Illustrated by Charles Tang

ALBERT WHITMAN & Company
Morton Grove, Illinois

Library of Congress Cataloging-in-Publication Data
Warner, Gertrude Chandler, 1890-1979
The dinosaur mystery/created by Gertrude Chandler Warner;
illustrated by Charles Tang.
p. cm. — (The boxcar children mysteries)
Summary: When the Aldens go to the Pickering Natural
History Museum to assist with the opening of a dinosaur exhibit,
their work is hampered by a series of mysterious happenings.
ISBN 0-8075-1603-1 (hardcover).
ISBN 0-8075-1604-X (paperback).
[1. Museums–Fiction. 2. Mystery and detective stories.]
I. Tang, Charles, ill. II. Title. III. Series:
Warner, Gertrude Chandler, 1890-
Boxcar children mysteries.
PZ7.W244Dg 1995   94-33214
[Fic]–dc20   CIP
                                          AC

Cover art by David Cunningham.

Contents

CHAPTER   PAGE

1. A Terrible Lizard   1
2. The Shadow Knows   14
3. Dark as Night   24
4. Someone Goes Down a Hole 37
5. A Tall "Tail" Mystery   50
6. No Bones About It   62
7. The Aldens Keep a Secret   74
8. Dig Those Bones   84
9. Lost in the Stars   98
10. Give the Dog a Bone   108

CHAPTER 1

A Terrible Lizard

Five suitcases, three good-sized ones and two small ones, stood next to three good-sized children and two small ones. The children's grandfather, James Alden, reached into the trunk of his car. They had just pulled up behind the Pickering Natural History Museum.

"Whoa!" Mr. Alden said as he dragged out a heavy box. "What's in here, Benny?"

"Rocks!" six-year-old Benny Alden announced as he helped his grandfather lift the box from the trunk.

"My goodness, Benny," twelve-year-old Jessie Alden teased, "I thought you were just bringing a small bag of your rocks."

"I couldn't decide, Jessie, so I brought all of them," Benny told his oldest sister. "Mr. and Mrs. Diggs can help me make them into a *real* rock collection!"

"Do they know about birds' nests, too?" Soo Lee asked her cousin Violet Alden.

"They know all about birds' nests, too. And fossils and dinosaurs and all kinds of things." She took her seven-year-old cousin by the hand.

Soo Lee smiled at Violet. The Aldens were part of her adopted family now. They were cousins of her parents, Joe and Alice Alden.

Mr. Alden closed the trunk of the car. "Well, children, I know the Pickering Museum will have a dinosaur skeleton or two and a few other things you children are going to like." Mr. Alden and Henry moved the suitcases next to the side entrance to the museum, which was closed at this hour. "Now, let's see. Where's that buzzer Emma and Archie told me to ring for the night watchman?"

"Here it is!" Soo Lee cried.

"Then give it a ring," Mr. Alden told her.

Soo Lee pressed, then pressed again. The Aldens could hear the bell echoing inside the museum. Soon they saw a light moving along the dark hall.

Benny and Soo Lee pressed their faces against the glass door.

"Benny," Soo Lee whispered. "Can you see it? Can you see the dinosaur?"

Before Benny could answer, a large figure blocked the door.

"Museum's closed!" the Aldens heard a man yell from inside.

Benny rang the bell this time. The guard aimed his flashlight at the Aldens.

"I said the museum's closed!" the man repeated. "It doesn't open until ten tomorrow."

Before the Aldens could explain why they were there, the man disappeared.

"I'm going to drive around the block to the Diggses' apartment," Mr. Alden said. "Maybe they forgot to tell the guard when we were arriving."

Mr. Alden drove off, and the Alden children sat down on their suitcases to wait.

"Here," Violet said to Soo Lee. "You can lean against me. Soon we'll be inside the Diggses' apartment with our own beds to sleep in. Tomorrow there will be plenty of time for dinosaurs."

Soo Lee nodded. She hugged the small teddy bear the Aldens had given her as a present when she'd arrived from Korea.

Benny tried to cover a yawn. "*I'm* not tired. I want to see the big old dinosaur that's inside this museum!"

Fourteen-year-old Henry yawned too. "Well, I don't think that dinosaur is going anywhere tonight, Benny."

Benny leaned up against the door again. When he did, a loud alarm began to buzz over and over. The children covered their ears to muffle the terrible sound.

"What's going on?" Henry yelled over the racket.

"Somebody's here!" Benny yelled back.

The museum door whooshed open. A tall man in a uniform and hat waved his flashlight over the children like a spotlight. Next to him, a large German shepherd pulled hard on a leash and growled at the children.

"I told you," the man began. "The museum's closed, and now you've set off the alarm!"

"I did?" Benny asked, surprised that he had caused all this ruckus.

The man pushed a button on the wall. The awful alarm finally stopped, but the dog's growling did not.

Benny usually liked dogs, even big ones. They reminded him of the Aldens' own wonderful dog, Watch. But Benny would rather have come face to face with a live dinosaur than this big dog!

"Down, Nosey!" the guard ordered.

"Nice dog," Jessie said in her sweet voice. "He's a watchdog. Just like our dog, Watch."

Jessie's soothing voice seemed to calm the animal. He stopped growling and began to sniff at the children.

"I bet he smells Watch's fur on our clothes," Henry explained to the guard. "We

couldn't bring him on this trip. Mr. and Mrs. Diggs don't have room for our whole family *and* our dog."

The guard gave the children a puzzled look. "You know Mr. and Mrs. Diggs? They are on the Board of Directors of the Pickering Museum!"

"They invited us to help set up the Dino World exhibit," Jessie explained politely. "They're friends of Grandfather's. They were looking for volunteers to help out."

The guard smacked his forehead. "Say, now I know what you're talking about! Mrs. Diggs did say something yesterday about meeting you with the loading cart tonight. Forgot all about it, I did. Even wrote myself a note since I'm always forgetting things, but — oops — I lost the note!"

The Alden children felt better now.

"I didn't mean to scare you," the man said in a much friendlier voice. "I'm Pete, Pete Lawlor. And this is our watchdog, Nosey. He's friendly when he knows you."

A phone rang in the distance, and Nosey's ears pricked up.

Pete Lawlor went off to answer the phone while the children gently stroked Nosey. He sniffed at the children's shoes, their suitcases, and their clothes.

"That was Mrs. Diggs on the phone," Pete said when he came back. "She told me to put your suitcases on this cart and bring you straight up to the apartment. I bet you don't know how we're going to get there."

"Through a tunnel?" Soo Lee guessed.

"Grandfather told us about the tunnel before we got here," Henry explained.

"Shucks!" Pete said. He pushed the cart down the dim hall past a wall of television screens that showed different rooms of the museum. "I wanted to surprise you. Just work people from the gas company and a few museum people use the tunnel. It runs underneath the museum and the apartment building across the way. That's where Mr. and Mrs. Diggs live. There's an entrance over this way," Pete said. "Straight through Africa."

Trailing behind Pete and Nosey, the children made their way through a large hall lit only by an exit sign. Up ahead were six huge humps.

Henry felt Soo Lee's hand squeeze his own. "Are those dinosaurs?" she asked.

"Not exactly," Henry answered. "Here, up you go." He gave her a boost up to his shoulders. "See?"

"Elephants!" Soo Lee exclaimed.

The cart squeaked to a stop when Pete reached a doorway. He pulled a crumpled map from his pocket. "Let's see, is it this door or the one over there?" he mumbled to himself.

The children looked at each other, puzzled. For a museum guard, Pete Lawlor didn't seem to know his way around very well.

"Let's try Entomology," he said.

"Ento what?" Soo Lee and Benny repeated together.

"Entomology," Jessie said. "Where they study bugs, I think."

Sure enough, when Pete opened the door, the Aldens found themselves in a room full of insects, hundreds of them!

"Take a look at that one!" Pete said. His flashlight stopped in front of a glass display case standing apart from the others.

"Wow!" Benny cried when he got a closer look. "I'm glad it's not alive and crawling around." It was a crunchy-looking beetle nearly five inches long.

"It's a Goliath beetle from Africa," Pete said. "How'd you like to meet up with one of those?"

"I don't think I would," Violet answered.

"Me neither," Henry agreed.

"Maybe I would!" Benny said, but his voice trailed away. Suddenly he felt tired after all. He'd had enough bugs for one night.

Benny's big yawn was catching, and the other children began to yawn, too.

"If you think that's a scary critter, take a look at this one," Pete said. He beamed his flashlight across the room to another display case.

Henry pointed to his watch. "You know what, Pete? We had a long car trip with our grandfather. How about a tour another time instead?"

"Sure," Pete said. "I get carried away and forget what time it is. Now let's see if I can find the right door. Give me a minute."

Pete trotted off, jangling his keys. The children leaned on each other, too tired to think about being in a strange, dark room full of bugs!

Just as their eyes began to adjust to the dim light, they heard the alarm scream again. Nosey bolted out of the bug room, his toenails clicking against the marble floors.

Soo Lee held on to Violet, and Benny stayed close to Jessie.

"Wait here," Henry said, racing after Nosey. "I'm going to see what set off that alarm. This time it wasn't us."

"I want to go, too," Benny said, half scared and half excited.

Leaving the cart behind, the other children covered their ears and followed Henry.

"Look, somebody went in there!" Benny pointed to a door.

Henry pulled it open.

The children jumped back. Inside the huge, dim room was a giant dinosaur skeleton with a jaw big enough to eat a tree — or a person! Shadows loomed on the wall.

Suddenly the children heard panting, then keys jangling. But they couldn't tell where the noises were coming from.

"Hey, how did you kids get in here?" Pete Lawlor said next. "I'm afraid it's off-limits without Dr. Pettibone here to let you in. Even Mr. and Mrs. Diggs are careful not to upset Titus by coming in here without him."

"Benny thought he saw somebody sneak in here," Henry explained, "so we just followed. We thought maybe it was you."

Pete shook his head. "No way! Titus Pettibone is the head of the fossil department, and nobody comes in here without his say-so. He doesn't want anything to happen to *T rex* here. This *Tyrannosaurus* is going to be the main attraction when Dino World opens. Titus has been working on this skeleton his whole life, and. . . ."

Pete forgot what he was saying. Instead, he beamed his flashlight up and down the skeleton as he walked around the huge creature. "I don't get too much of a chance to see

T rex myself. What a beast! No wonder they called some dinosaurs terrible lizards."

"Come on, you two," Jessie said. "Let's go find Mr. and Mrs. Diggs."

The children headed toward the exit. The door was about to click shut when Violet stopped.

"Where's Pete?" she asked.

The children turned around. There were two dinosaurs in the room now, the huge real skeleton and the even larger shadow that covered the wall and ceiling. And Pete had forgotten all about the Aldens as he kept flashing his light over the dinosaur skeleton.

"Pete! Pete!" Henry's voice echoed.

Finally Pete pulled away from the dinosaur, nearly tripping over its tailbones.

"Sorry, kids," he apologized. "I just wanted another look. It seems bigger and more amazing at night."

With Pete and Nosey leading the way, the children filed out of the dinosaur room, and did not see another shadow moving slowly across the wall.

CHAPTER 2

The Shadow Knows

Pete deposited the children at Mr. and Mrs. Diggs's. "It's nice to be in a normal apartment," Benny said.

An older gray-haired couple smiled at the children.

"Not too normal." Grandfather Alden laughed. "Just take a peek in the other rooms."

The children stuck their heads in the living room. Every inch of it was crammed with amazing things. Several animal skulls hung on the wall. Stuffed animals and birds of all kinds filled each corner. Benny looked admiringly at a collection of old snakeskins.

"We're so lucky to be living and working at such a fine museum," Mrs. Diggs told Benny. "We get a lot of its leftovers."

"I like leftovers!" Benny announced.

"You can't eat those leftovers, Benny," Archie Diggs said. "But Emma and I made you folks some sandwiches from our roast chicken dinner."

"Leftover chicken sandwiches are my favorites," Benny said.

Laughing and talking, the Aldens sat down at the Diggses' kitchen table to eat sandwiches and to make plans for the next day.

"Now tomorrow morning, first thing, I'll give you a quick tour of the museum before it opens," Archie Diggs began. "You'll meet Eve Skyler, who's head of the planetarium. And the day after, you'll work with our famous fossil scientist, Titus Pettibone."

Mrs. Diggs put down her teacup when she noticed the Aldens frowning. "What is it, children? Is something wrong?"

"Mr. Bones might get mad at us," Soo Lee said. "The man with the flashlight told us."

"Told you what?" Mr. Diggs asked.

"That Titus Pettibone doesn't let anybody near the dinosaur room and, well . . . that's where we wanted to help out," Henry explained.

"We know you do," Mrs. Diggs said. "That's the whole reason we asked you here. Why, with the Dino World opening just a week away, Titus knows he can't do every thing himself."

"Not to mention all the problems we've been having around here lately," Archie said. "Our alarm system seems to be acting up. And our new night watchman, Pete — a nice young man, mind you — still needs a lot of supervision. He just started on the job."

"Now, Archie, you and Emma shouldn't worry," Mr. Alden said. "Once Titus learns how careful these children are, he'll be glad to have them on board."

"Thanks, James," Mrs. Diggs said. Mr. Alden stood up to go. He would be back for the opening of Dino World. Mrs. Diggs handed him his hat and scarf. "I know your grandchildren and your grandniece will be a big help."

After walking their grandfather to the door to say good-bye, Henry, Jessie, and Violet rejoined Benny and Soo Lee in the kitchen. When they got there, the food had been cleared away, and in the middle of the table was Benny's rock box. Benny was sitting next to Mrs. Diggs and explaining where he had found each and every rock. "This one came from the stream next to where we lived in our boxcar," Benny told Mrs. Diggs. "I'm saving it forever and ever."

Mrs. Diggs put on her glasses for a closer look. "This one's a nice piece of black shale, Benny. Now tell me, what's in that jar?"

Benny slowly took out a mayonnaise jar full of shiny dead insects.

"Your cicadas, Benny!" Jessie cried. "You brought your dead cicadas, too?"

Benny held up the jar as proudly as if it held gold nuggets. "A whole jar full!" he told Mr. and Mrs. Diggs. "They fall out of the big tree in our backyard every summer, and

I save them. I don't think they live long."

"You'll make a good scientist," Mr. Diggs told Benny. "Adult cicadas only live a few weeks, but they sing up a storm for those few weeks. They look quite nice in that jar too. Good place for them. This week, I'll take you to the Entomology Room."

"Entomology is the study of . . ." Mrs. Diggs began to explain to the children.

"Bugs!" Benny and Soo Lee shouted together.

"Pete told us when he took us to the bug room," Violet said.

Mrs. Diggs looked surprised. "Took you to the bug room? Whatever for?"

"He thought it was a shortcut to get to your apartment," Henry said. "But we came here a different way, over by the dinosaur room."

"You were in the dinosaur room, too?" Mr. Diggs asked. "How on earth did you get inside? I hope Pete didn't fool with that lock. He's still finding his way around, I'm afraid."

"I was afraid, too," Soo Lee said, biting

her lip. "The big dinosaur made big shadows way, way up."

Mrs. Diggs patted Soo Lee on the shoulder. "Well, you needn't be afraid. We'll get Titus to give you a tour during the day. My goodness, I wonder what Pete was doing over on that side of the museum at this late hour? Well, let's get you all off to bed and figure this out in the morning. You children have a big day ahead."

"And a big dinosaur ahead, too!" Benny said in an excited voice.

With Mr. and Mrs. Diggs leading the way, the children followed the couple up a short set of stairs to two rooms off a landing.

"Now that Dino World is nearly ready," Mrs. Diggs explained, "we've had to move a lot of things wherever there's room. You'll even find a few interesting things in these guest quarters. Usually we have scientists and museum people staying there, so it's all decorated with specimens from the museum. I hope you children don't mind."

The children stepped inside a small room

with a second room connecting to it. Just like the rest of the apartment, these rooms were jammed with all kinds of objects from the museum.

Mr. Diggs pulled down a tiny, stuffed animal with huge eyes to show Benny and Soo Lee. "Now this little fellow is a marmoset monkey. He's about thirty years old. There was no room for him at the museum, so we adopted him."

Benny stroked the stuffed animal, which looked as if it had just jumped down from a tree.

"I can move some of these things to a closet," Mr. Diggs offered. "If they bother you."

"Oh, but we like all this stuff," Benny said. "Soo Lee and I take walks and find things — like my cicadas. I keep them in my room."

Soo Lee showed Mrs. Diggs her special box. "Violet and I found it in the woods. It's a bird's nest."

"A fine hummingbird's nest," Mrs. Diggs said as she turned back the covers on the beds. "You Aldens are all such curious children. I know our staff will enjoy showing you the Pickering's wonderful treasures."

In no time, the Alden children were fast asleep, all except Jessie. Without Watch at the foot of her bed, she couldn't fall asleep right away. The guest room faced the street, and the street lamps and traffic sounds kept her awake.

"Too noisy," she whispered to herself as she smoothed her covers, then her pillow, and tried to get comfortable.

"Too bright," she whispered more loudly. She finally got out of bed and went to the window.

The big museum, straight ahead, was completely dark. Jessie watched the cars go by and the traffic lights change from green, to yellow, to red. Even at night, the city streets were so bright. Jessie reached for the windowshade to darken the room. As she did, she heard a faint buzzing sound in the distance. Was it traffic or a radio or a television or just ringing in her ears?

"I wish Watch were here," Jessie said to herself as she pulled down the shade. Then

she stopped. Why was a light moving across some of the museum windows?

"Huh!" she cried suddenly. There was a large dark shape in the tall windows across the way. Jessie stepped back.

Violet mumbled from her bed. "What's the matter, Jessie?" she asked in a sleepy voice.

Jessie squinted, but the light in the museum was gone, taking with it the shadowy forms.

"Nothing," Jessie whispered to Violet. "It's nothing."

She got into bed and pulled the covers up to her chin. The room was still too bright. On the night table, Jessie could see the small mouse skull that had looked so delicate and pretty in the light. And over on a bookshelf, the glass eyes of the stuffed marmoset monkey seemed to be watching her. Jessie pulled the covers over her face, but quite a few minutes passed before she stopped seeing the huge black outline in the museum window across the way — the moving shadow of the long-dead dinosaur!

CHAPTER 3

Dark as Night

"Is it okay to have another muffin?" Benny whispered to Jessie the next morning at breakfast.

"Here, take mine," Jessie told him.

"How come you're not hungry?" Henry asked his sister.

Jessie yawned. "I'm more tired than hungry. I had the worst time falling asleep last night. First I was too hot, then it was too light in the room, then I thought I heard an alarm."

Just as Jessie said this, Mr. Diggs walked

into the kitchen. "You must have heard a car alarm. They go off at all hours for no reason in a big city like this."

Mrs. Diggs came back from the pantry with more food for the children. "Pete left a message on the phone machine that everything was quiet all night."

At this, Jessie looked up. "Was he sure? I saw lights in the windows of the dinosaur room last night, right after I heard that alarm sound. Maybe it was Pete."

Mr. Diggs came around with more orange juice for everyone. "Oh, I doubt it. Pete spends the night on the other side of the museum at the control desk. We have remote cameras so he can keep an eye on the whole museum from there."

"But I saw a shadow in the dinosaur room, just like the ones we saw when Pete first showed us the *Tyrannosaurus* last night," Jessie explained. "Somebody was in there!"

Mrs. Diggs shook her head and smiled. "Well, with an old building like this you get all kinds of reflections from the traffic, lights, and such."

The children finished breakfast quickly. They couldn't wait to get started.

"Guess what?" Benny asked his sisters and brother. "Mr. Diggs is going to give me a real sorting box for my rocks and real museum signs — little ones — so I can label my collection."

"And I'm going to give Soo Lee a display box for her bird's nest," Mrs. Diggs told the children.

"And guess what else?" Soo Lee asked in an excited voice. "Benny and I are going to make a museum in the boxcar in Grandfather's backyard when we get home! Mr. Diggs said Pete will give us real museum tickets to use when people come to *our* museum!"

Mr. Diggs laughed. "Well, first you have to come to *our* museum to get some ideas. Let's go!"

That morning the museum was flooded with daylight. The five Aldens looked everywhere at once. In one hall, they passed a giant Viking boat with the longest oars the children had ever seen. A couple of rooms away, a giant whale hung from the ceiling, and fingers of light made it seem as if everything were underwater.

"First stop, the planetarium," Mr. Diggs told the excited children. "Eve Skyler, our director, needs a lot of help there."

Mrs. Diggs met everyone at the planetarium entrance. "I forgot to mention that this is a big surprise for Eve," she said in a low voice. "She's been so upset with all the confusion around here. And who can blame her? All this dust and nails and banging, and with most of our staff busy with Dino World, she's had to cancel a number of sky shows."

Mr. Diggs unlocked the door, and everyone stepped inside.

"Oooo!" the Aldens gasped as they stepped into the darkened room.

The only light came from hundreds of stars sprinkled across the ceiling. They could hear a woman's deep voice talking from somewhere in the room.

"And over in the West is Venus," the voice was saying.

The children tried to see who was speaking, but it was much too dark.

"What on earth?" Mr. Diggs said.

"Or what in heaven?" Jessie said.

Benny asked, "How did it get to be nighttime? And how come we're outside all of a sudden?"

"It does feel exactly as if we're outside." Violet whispered. "Listen, there are crickets!"

Violet was right. The sound of crickets filled the air just as if the children were in their own backyard looking at the stars.

"It's magic," Violet whispered. "Like someone turned the morning into night and opened the roof to show us the stars."

"Look." Henry pointed to the lower part of the curved ceiling. "The moon is rising in the East."

"It's just a movie of stars and the moon," Henry explained. "And the person who was talking is just a recording, and so were the crickets."

Mr. Diggs, who had been searching for the light switch inside the planetarium, called out, "Now get ready, children. I'll make it daytime again. One . . . two . . . three!"

With that, the light went on, and the sky, the stars, and the moon all disappeared. The Aldens found themselves standing in a room that looked like a round movie theater with rows of seats arranged in circles.

And in one of those seats was Pete Lawlor!

"Pete!" Mr. Diggs cried. "What are you doing here? I thought you were off your shift by now. And why was the sky show running?"

Pete seemed surprised to see everyone standing there. "Uh . . . yeah. Dr. Skyler left a message and . . . well I thought I heard something suspicious in here when I was coming off my shift, and so I . . . I thought I'd better check it out. Then I figured, what if someone got at all this expensive equipment in here, so I decided to try it out."

"Well, goodness, Pete, that's why we have a camera security system, so you don't have to be everywhere at once," Mrs. Diggs said. "And where's Nosey?"

Pete shifted from one foot to the other. "I left him with the morning guard, the way I usually do when I sign off. I'd best be going."

With that, Pete rushed by the Aldens without so much as a hello. When everyone went inside, they found Pete's hat on one of the seats along with his flashlight.

Mr. Diggs sighed and shook his head. "That young man is going to leave the museum unlocked one of these days or damage something valuable, and then where will we be, Emma? I'm almost tempted to let him go, but we've never had a guard here who loved the museum so much. Imagine, running the sky show at this hour just to check the equipment!"

"What is this machine anyway?" Benny asked. "Why is it full of holes?"

"It's a special kind of projector, Benny. When the light goes through all those little holes, it makes stars on the ceiling," Mrs. Diggs explained.

Benny, who liked any kind of machine, took a closer look. When he did, he heard a sharp voice.

"Don't touch that, little boy! Leave it alone!"

Everyone whirled around to see who was shouting at Benny. Up in a windowed office overlooking the planetarium stood a woman with short, straight, brown hair. She was shaking her finger at everyone below.

"Eve, my goodness!" Mr. Diggs called up. "It's Emma and me, and we've brought our guests. Please come down to meet them."

A minute or two later, the woman joined everyone. "I'm sorry, Archie. You know the planetarium doesn't open until ten, even to school groups," she said. She looked at the Aldens as if they were trespassing. "In any case, we can't open today with all the confusion."

"We realize that, Eve," Mr. Diggs said. "Pete mentioned you'd left a message at the security desk. Not that Pete was any kind of help in here watching the sky show just now."

The woman's eyebrows shot up. "Watching the sky show? Today? Why of all things! That's no help at all. I simply called the security desk to ask them for the hundredth time to fix the lock. The people keep wandering in here with their lunches and their coffee cups and their . . . and now this school group you brought in. It's just *too* much."

"Now, now, Eve," Mrs. Diggs said, patting the woman's shoulder. "That's why we're here. This isn't a school group. It's the Alden family, and they've come to help us out. Children, this is our planetarium director, Dr. Eve Skyler."

Henry, who was standing closest to Dr. Skyler, smiled and put out his hand, but the woman didn't seem to notice.

"I'm sure I don't need children underfoot with everything I have to do," Dr. Skyler said. "Just look around. There are buckets of paint the painters just left here. Don't even ask me how they got into my planetarium in the first place! They leave their lunch bags and soda cans lying around. Everything is in a mess."

Jessie spoke up. "But we're not regular visitors, Dr. Skyler. We could clean up the planetarium in no time so that you could keep

running your sky shows. That's why we came."

Again, the woman ignored Jessie and the other Aldens. Instead, she turned her attention to Mr. and Mrs. Diggs.

"Emma, if you and Archie think I can't run the planetarium, then you should just tell me, and I'll resign immediately."

"There, there, Eve," Mrs. Diggs said in a soothing voice. "We want you to do what you do best, which is to teach everyone about the stars and the sky. And you can't do it with all this rubble and noise."

Mr. Diggs signaled for the children. "We've brought five pairs of helping hands here to move the construction materials out of here and do a cleanup. They've worked in museums and old houses, so they know how to be careful around valuable things, I promise you. This will free up your time to get the sky shows up and running tomorrow."

Dr. Skyler didn't agree. "Tomorrow! That isn't possible even if we had five adult workers here, let alone these children!"

Jessie spoke up. "Just try us and see how we do."

With several pairs of eyes on her, Dr. Skyler nodded. "All right, but mind you, you'll have to be careful around the projector. Don't go stirring up any dust near there. The cleaning things are through that door. And put everything back in the same place it came from."

"We know." Henry led the other children toward the storage room.

"Boy, she sure doesn't want us around," Benny said.

"She will when we make this place spic-and-span," Henry said. He handed out work gloves, trash bags, and dust cloths to everyone.

As the children got themselves organized for a big cleaning job, they couldn't help thinking about Pete, too.

"It sure seemed strange that he was just sitting in the planetarium watching a movie so early in the morning, don't you think, Jessie?" Henry asked.

"Maybe he's absentminded," Jessie answered. "He doesn't seem too organized."

"Not like us!" Benny said proudly as he whizzed around pushing a big broom in circles.

"Well, you children look like a regular cleaning team," Mrs. Diggs said when the Aldens came back into the planetarium with all the cleaning gear. "I know you'll do a wonderful job."

Mr. Diggs had a stack of posters in his hand. "If you finish up here this morning, you can take these Dino World posters and put them up around the area this afternoon. It's about our big opening next week."

Before the children could even get a look at the posters, Dr. Skyler stepped between them and Mr. Diggs. "If they're going to help me out, Archie, they won't have time for putting up posters. I'm afraid those will have to wait." With that, Dr. Skyler shooed Mr. and Mrs. Diggs out the door so the Aldens could get down to work.

CHAPTER 4

Someone Goes Down a Hole

"Whew!" Henry said several hours later when the children finally finished moving the construction materials to the hall. "Dr. Skyler wasn't kidding. That sure was a lot to clear out of there."

Jessie pushed back her braid for the umpteenth time. "Not to mention just plain old cleaning. We still have to vacuum, wash, dust, you name it."

"I name . . . lunch!" Benny piped up.

"I'm hungry, too," Soo Lee said. "Is it lunchtime, Jessie?"

"It sure is," Jessie answered. "Dr. Skyler took a break, so we might as well do the same."

"Let's eat at the museum cafeteria," Violet suggested. "Mrs. Diggs said she would leave coupons for us there for anything we wanted."

When the Aldens got to the busy museum cafeteria, chicken fricassee was the special of the day. The children took trays and got on the long line. While they were waiting, Jessie felt a tap on her shoulder.

"So you couldn't finish the job after all, could you? Had to rush off so you could go help Dino World," Dr. Skyler said. "I don't know what Emma and Archie were thinking, bringing a bunch of children to work in a museum."

Jessie put down her tray. "Sorry. We were only taking a lunch break. We finished moving all the construction things out, just like you told us. This afternoon we'll do the real cleaning. I'm sure we can finish so you can start up the sky shows tomorrow."

This didn't calm down Dr. Skyler. "Not

if you're taking lunch breaks all the time."

The woman stomped out of the cafeteria.

The younger children looked at Jessie and Henry. What was this all about?

"Oh, bother," Henry said. "I guess we'd better have a quick lunch and get right back."

After eating quickly, the children headed back to the planetarium. When they arrived upstairs, they saw Dr. Skyler pushing a loaded cart.

Henry ran ahead. "Wait! Wait! Why are you moving that stuff back inside?" he asked Dr. Skyler. "We put it all down the hall next to the Dumpster the way you told us."

Dr. Skyler whirled around, startled by Henry's voice.

"Don't be ridiculous," she said. "I was just returning to get something."

Jessie checked one of the black trash bags. "But I know I put this bag in the Dumpster down the hall where you said."

"Never mind what you did and what I said," Dr. Skyler snapped. "I need you to finish up in here. There's still plenty of rub-bish to take out, not to mention the vacuuming and cleaning. You've got a full afternoon's work here. This list has all the jobs left to do. Here, take it."

With that, Dr. Skyler left. When the children went inside the planetarium, they got a big surprise.

"Somebody moved things back here!" Henry cried. "Those are the same tool boxes we moved out of here before lunch."

"We practically have to start over again," Jessie said.

Eve Skyler was right. It did take the Aldens the whole afternoon to get through the work list. They were too tired and too busy to figure out how so much of the construction rubbish wound up back inside the planetarium instead of outside where it belonged.

This setback didn't stop the Aldens. They were going to finish up no matter what was going on with Dr. Skyler. They swept, and they vacuumed. They washed, and they dusted. And by the time they were done with all of it, the museum was closed, and it was dark outside.

"We haven't had a breath of air all day,"

Jessie said. "Let's take the long way back to the apartment and walk outside, okay?"

"Good idea," Henry agreed. "I could use some fresh air after all that dust and dirt."

The children left a note telling Dr. Skyler they had finished.

"Phew, I'm glad we're done with that," Jessie said when everyone reached the sidewalk. "It feels good to be outside. I guess tomorrow we'll put up some of those posters Mr. Diggs showed us. That'll be a lot more fun. And Dr. Pettibone will be back. Maybe we can work with him instead."

The children walked along slowly, happy to be outdoors for a change. If they hadn't been so tired, they would have enjoyed looking in the shop and restaurant windows just like all the city people with a free night ahead.

"Maybe tomorrow night we could eat in one of these cozy restaurants," Jessie told the younger children, who were trailing behind. "A city like this has so many different places to eat. Wouldn't you like to try one of them, Benny?"

For once, Benny didn't have anything to say, even about eating. Something more important than food had caught his attention.

"Hey, did you see that?" Benny pointed across the street.

"I saw it! I saw it, too!" Soo Lee jumped up and down. "Somebody went down a hole in the street. Just like a rabbit!"

The older children looked at each other. Whomever Soo Lee and Benny had seen had disappeared.

"You mean where that manhole is over there?" Jessie asked.

"And somebody just went down it," Benny said.

Henry looked up and down the street. "Are you sure, Benny? I don't see any power company workers around or anything. Pete mentioned they sometimes use the underground tunnel to check on things. Was the person wearing a hard hat?"

"No," Benny said. "He was wearing a white beard."

The children stared at the manhole. The outer rim of the cover was sticking up as if

someone had been too rushed to pull it tight. Then a car drove right over it, and the manhole cover locked into place.

"Whoever went down there better be careful about coming up again," Benny said.

"He could get squished!" Soo Lee said.

Now the Aldens were full of curiosity and not a bit tired anymore.

Benny kept staring at the manhole cover. "Hey, I have a good idea! Let's find out who's down there. The person has to come out somewhere."

"Okay," Henry agreed. "I'll tell you what. You and I will go back into the museum to that entrance Pete took us through last night to get to the passageway."

"And Violet and Soo Lee and I will go to the door at the other end in the apartment house," Jessie said, suddenly enjoying the idea of an adventure.

"We'll see who finds the disappearing man first," Violet said with a laugh.

"One, two, three, go!" Benny shouted.

The Aldens split up. Jessie, Violet, and Soo Lee headed to the apartment building.

Henry and Benny raced back to the museum.

"Why would anyone go down under the street at nighttime?" Violet asked Jessie.

Jessie winked at Violet. "Maybe Benny and Soo Lee didn't really see anything," she whispered. "But let's pretend anyway. They're having fun, and so am I."

"Okay." Violet turned back to Soo Lee. "Let's see if we can find the person before Benny and Henry do."

When the girls reached the apartment building, the doorman let them in the back way.

"Maybe the man is in the tunnel," Soo Lee said when they didn't see signs of anyone in the back hall.

"Okay, okay," Jessie said. "Let's check." She turned the doorknob to the passageway door, but it was locked. "I guess you have to have the key like Pete did. Let's just wait for Benny and Henry to come back."

Across the street, back in the museum, Henry and Benny banged on the side entrance door. Again, they heard a voice: "The museum is closed! Come back tomorrow."

They banged again, and this time Pete and Nosey came running.

"Oh, it's you and Benny," Pete said. "Sorry it took so long, but Nosey thought he heard something down at the other end of the museum."

"He did?" Benny said. "Well, guess what? We saw somebody go down the manhole in the street. We came to find out if the person came into the museum through the underground part."

Pete laughed. "Well, if somebody did, the person is stuck down there. You have to have a key for any of the doors that lead off of it. And if you had a key, then you sure wouldn't need to go down the manhole to get inside the museum or apartment. You could just walk in the front door!"

This didn't stop Benny. He was ready for an adventure, and he was going to have one. "What if somebody wants to sneak in a secret way? Maybe Nosey did hear somebody."

Pete patted Benny's curly head. "Tell you

what, Benny. I'll take you down to the passageway myself, and we'll check it out.
That's my job. First let me take a look at the
television screens to make sure everything is
A-OK in the rest of the museum."

Benny and Henry walked quickly to the
guard booth. This time Pete let Benny inside
so he could get a look at the screens that
showed different rooms in the museum.

"See any prowlers or anything suspicious
on any of those televisions?" Pete asked
Benny.

"Just me!" Benny said with a laugh. He
made faces at the camera that was pointing
right at him from the ceiling of the guard
booth.

"That's a dangerous face if I ever saw one!"
Pete joked.

Henry checked out the row of televisions,
too. "This is pretty neat," he said. "Do you
ever see anything on the screens?"

"Not so far," Pete said. "It's pretty dull.
Once in a while I get excited when I see a
person on the screen, but it always turns out

to be somebody who works here. I still like walking around, not just watching these televisions the whole night."

"Hey, why is this screen dark?" Henry asked.

Pete explained, "Oh, that one's been on the blink for the past couple of weeks. It's the screen for Dino World. We can't seem to get the camera working right. Not that it matters. Titus Pettibone is a better guard of that place than any of the real guards."

"But who watches over the place now that he's away? Don't forget, last night it was unlocked," Henry said.

Pete looked away. "Oh, uh, well . . . maybe one of the work crew got tired of asking Titus for the key and taped the latch to go in and out. There's a lot of work in there that still needs doing before opening day."

Benny was getting impatient. "Is there a television screen for the passageway? If we don't get down there, the person I saw will be gone."

"The passageway isn't rigged up to the

remote cameras," Pete said. "Only Mr. and Mrs. Diggs and a few other museum people ever use it. Or utility people when they check the water and gas lines. Anyway, the doors down there and the service elevator all lock from both sides."

Just as Pete had said, the passageway was deserted when they got there.

"Rats! We took too long," Benny said. "The person got away."

"Guess so, Benny," Pete said. "Want to help me out on my post tonight? Maybe there will be some other kind of excitement."

Benny shook his head. "Nope. We missed it."

"Well, so long, Pete. Thanks for checking things out for us," Henry said. "Sorry to bother you."

Pete unlocked the service elevator for the boys. "It's no bother. As I said, it's pretty dull around here."

But Pete was wrong. Things were not pretty dull around the museum. In fact, they were about to get pretty exciting.

CHAPTER 5

A Tall "Tail" Mystery

The next morning when the Aldens got up, the apartment was empty.

"Gee, I wonder where Mr. and Mrs. Diggs went," Henry said when he realized the Aldens were alone in the apartment. "Today's the day for us to meet Dr. Pettibone."

Jessie found a message on the kitchen counter and read it aloud.

Dear Aldens,
We're sorry not to have breakfast with you. There's juice in the refrigerator and coffee cake

on the counter. Help yourselves. Titus Pettibone
had an emergency this morning when he arrived
from his trip, and we had to see him right away.
Please meet us in the dinosaur hall.

                 Emma and Archie Diggs

"Wow, an emergency!" Benny cried.

In no time, the Aldens had eaten and were
on their way to the museum, racing down
the sidewalk as fast as they could. They
showed their visitor passes at the museum
entrance, then zoomed by the Viking boats
and the whale without stopping. Outside the
dinosaur hall a small, noisy crowd of people
had formed. The children couldn't get
through.

"I can't see," Benny said. "There are too
many people."

"Where's the dinosaur?" Soo Lee asked. "I
can't see either."

Henry and Jessie, who were the tallest,
stood on their tiptoes to see what was going
on.

"The door's roped off," Henry explained
to the younger children. "It looks like Mr.

and Mrs. Diggs are talking to the police!"

Benny couldn't stand the suspense. Being small, he squeezed himself through the crowd. "Excuse me. Excuse me," he repeated until he reached the Diggs.

He stopped. His eyebrows shot up. "Hey, that's the man with the white beard!" he cried.

But just then Emma Diggs spotted Benny and came over to get him. "Goodness, Benny. How did you make it through this mob? I was just about to call the apartment to have you take the freight elevator and get off right in back at the dinosaur hall. I'll have Pete fetch the other children. He's about to go off duty anyway. Pete? Pete?"

Pete was so busy walking around and around the dinosaur hall with Nosey that he didn't hear Mrs. Diggs right away. Finally she went to get him.

"Hey, Benny," Pete said when Mrs. Diggs finally brought him over. "I guess I was wrong last night about things being pretty dull around here."

Benny couldn't stand the suspense. "What happened, anyway?" he asked.

"Let's get the other kids, and I'll tell you everything we know," Pete said. "Coming through! Make way! Coming through!"

When they saw Nosey pulling at the leash, people in the crowd moved aside so Pete and Benny could get by and rejoin Henry, Jessie, Violet, and Soo Lee.

Jessie leaned over to pet Nosey. "What's going on, Pete? Mrs. Diggs said there was an emergency."

Pete took off his guard hat and brushed back his hair. "You're not kidding there's an emergency — a missing bone emergency! When Titus Pettibone arrived this morning and checked the *Tyrannosaurus* skeleton, parts of the jawbone and tailbones were gone! Disappeared. This is the only museum with a complete skeleton — or *was* the only one."

Benny hopped from one foot to the other and tried to get Pete's attention. "But that's the man I saw last night going down the hole in the street," he said, pointing to the man with the white beard.

Pete gave Benny a friendly punch on the shoulder. "Oh that! Maybe your eyes were fooling you. That's Dr. Pettibone! He just got back from the airport this morning and came straight here."

This didn't stop Benny. "Wait — Soo Lee saw him, too. Come on Soo Lee, let's go find the man."

Soo Lee hadn't been in the Alden family too long, but already she liked adventures and mysteries and emergencies just as much as her cousins. She followed right behind Benny. The two of them scooted through the crowd with Henry, Jessie, Violet, Pete, and Nosey trying to keep up.

When the crowd parted, Benny jumped up and down. "There's the man who went down the hole!"

"Benny is such a good detective," Jessie whispered to Violet, "but this time I wonder if he's right. Dr. Pettibone does have a white beard, but he looks so important and so serious, I'm sure he wouldn't be sneaking down a manhole."

"That *is* the man we saw," Soo Lee insisted

when she overheard Jessie. "Do you think he forgot his key and couldn't get in?"

Before Jessie could answer, Archie Diggs and the bearded man came over. The Aldens could see that the man was upset. He never once looked directly at the children.

"Titus, I would like you to meet James Alden's grandchildren, Henry, Jessie, Violet, Benny, and Soo Lee, his grandniece," Mr. Diggs began. "Children, this is our famous fossil expert, Dr. Pettibone."

The children all said their hellos, but Dr. Pettibone was too busy trying to keep Nosey from jumping on him. "Young man," he said to Pete, "get that dog out of here! It only adds to all this confusion."

"As I started to say, Titus, these are James Alden's . . ." Mrs. Diggs began until she noticed how upset Dr. Pettibone was. "Are you all right, Titus?" she asked. "I know you've had a great shock. I'll go get you some water. Maybe there's some way these children can help out. James Alden has told me many times how helpful they've been in emergencies. If nothing else, they can do some small things that need doing so you can focus on those missing bones."

"Missing bones?" Dr. Pettibone said, as if he didn't know anything about them. "Ah, yes. The missing bones."

Just then, two police officers stepped through the crowd. Mrs. Diggs turned to the children after Titus Pettibone and Archie Diggs went off to speak to the police. "You children will have to forgive Titus's manners today. He's simply beside himself. He can't seem to figure out what to do, poor man. This dinosaur is his whole life. Why, he went and called the newspapers before he called the police. Imagine!"

The children leaned their heads back to get a better look at the *Tyrannosaurus* skeleton. While it wasn't as scary during the day, the dinosaur was still plenty huge and plenty frightening, even without part of its big jawbone and some of its tailbones.

"Who would want a dinosaur bone anyway?" Henry asked.

"I sure would!" Benny answered before he realized what he'd said. "I mean if I found

one or they sold them in the museum shop."

This made Mrs. Diggs smile. "Don't worry, Benny. You don't look like a bone thief, if there was a thief, that is. The police wondered if perhaps somebody on the staff or work crew somehow disturbed the skeleton without meaning to and possibly broke the bones. Of course, no one's been in here since Titus was gone, so I'm probably wrong."

"We were here," Soo Lee announced. "The other night."

Jessie looked embarrassed. "It's true, Mrs. Diggs. Remember we told you we thought we saw someone — or Benny thought he did — so we came right in. The door wasn't even locked."

A police officer came up to Jessie. "Did I hear you say the dinosaur hall was unlocked the other night? You children were actually in here?"

"Yes, we were," Jessie confessed. "I mean, we didn't know we shouldn't come here. We heard a noise and thought we saw something, so we came to check."

The police officer looked very serious. "I see," she said. "Well, I'd like to take a statement from you. Now, please tell me how long you were here, how you got here, and so forth."

When Mrs. Diggs saw how upset Jessie looked, she spoke to the officer herself. "Lieutenant, all these children are friends of our family. They're here for a visit. If they were in the dinosaur hall the other night, it's because someone, perhaps a work person, left the door open. The children wouldn't touch a thing. They've been staying with us and wouldn't so much as use a spoon without asking for permission!"

This didn't stop the police officer. "That's very well and good, Mrs. Diggs, but this isn't an apartment, and there are valuable fossils missing, not a spoon. I must do my job. Anyone who was in or near this dinosaur hall in the last few days has to make a statement. That includes these children. I'm sorry."

"We don't mind," Violet said firmly. "We came in here because we thought we were chasing someone."

"Chasing someone?" the police officer asked. "Who were you chasing?"

"A shadow Benny saw," Soo Lee answered.

When she heard this, the police officer lost interest. "Oh, a *shadow*. Well, small children are always seeing shadows. My six-year-old nephew thinks the shadow of the tree branch outside his bedroom is a big snake."

This upset Benny so much, he couldn't be quiet. "It wasn't a snake I saw or a tree branch shaped like a snake. It was a *real* shadow that belonged to a real person. I chased it with my brother Henry, but it disappeared when we got inside here."

Soo Lee tilted her head back and looked up at the giant dinosaur skeleton. "Then we saw this skeleton all over the ceiling, all black and pointy with big teeth, from Pete's flashlight."

The officer took another look at Soo Lee. "You mean the night guard over there?" she said, pointing at Pete. "He was in here with you?"

Soo Lee nodded. "Not the whole time.

First we were in here by ourselves. I was scared. Then Pete came."

"I see, I see," the police officer said. "I have to talk to that fellow again. People keep telling me he's often in places where he shouldn't be. And despite several work orders, he never did arrange to get the remote security camera fixed in here."

"Dear, dear," Mrs. Diggs said after the officer went off to question Pete. "I'm afraid poor Pete is in for it." With that, Mrs. Diggs went off to join Mr. Diggs.

"Did I do okay, Jessie? Did I?" Soo Lee asked.

Jessie smoothed the little girl's shiny, black bangs. "Of course you did. We all told the truth, and that's always okay. The police have to interview everyone."

Violet came over to Jessie and spoke in a low voice. "One thing I'm not sure about is where Pete was when we were in here. Was he already inside or did he follow us in?"

The Aldens looked at each another. No one had an answer to that.

CHAPTER 6

No Bones About It

After all the excitement had died down, Mr. and Mrs. Diggs cleared everyone from the dinosaur hall. Only the Aldens and Dr. Pettibone were left.

"Now Titus," Mrs. Diggs began. "I know you must be very distracted by this terrible loss, not to mention losing a morning's work so close to the opening. This is the perfect time for the Aldens to pitch in."

"Who are the Aldens?" Dr. Pettibone had completely forgotten that he'd already met the children.

"Why, these children here, Titus. James Alden's family," Mrs. Diggs said. "They are very eager to work on the dinosaur exhibit."

"With my dinosaurs?" Dr. Pettibone said. "No, Emma, I don't think so. I plan to work alone right up until the opening, even if I have to stay up every night."

Soo Lee and Benny found it hard not to interrupt. They kept waiting for Mrs. Diggs and Dr. Pettibone to stop talking.

"Can I ask him about being in the manhole?" Benny asked Henry in a loud whisper.

When Dr. Pettibone overheard this, he stopped right in the middle of his sentence and turned away from the Aldens. "I simply can't do my work with all these children around, Emma. Send them away. Just send them away."

Mrs. Diggs sighed and motioned to the children to follow her out. When they reached the lobby, the children could see how upset Mrs. Diggs was.

"I know you are patient," Mrs. Diggs began. "Let me talk to Titus privately. I'll tell him about all the experience you children have had working with valuable things. He's so upset right now. Maybe this morning would be a good time to get the posters up now that the planetarium is straightened out. Archie left them on the table next to the sky show programs."

"We'll go get them and start right away, Mrs. Diggs," Henry said as they headed toward the planetarium. "Maybe Dr. Pettibone will be glad for some helping hands when we're done."

Dr. Skyler spotted the Aldens right away. "You're late," she said. "I suppose you couldn't wait to get to Dino World. As you can see, there's a huge crowd waiting to get into the planetarium. All the silly ruckus at Dino World made people want to come here instead."

Henry shifted from one foot to the other. "We didn't know you wanted us to work at the planetarium this morning. We finished the cleanup job last night, but if you need us in here, here we are!"

"I've already made other arrangements," Dr. Skyler snapped.

"Where are the Dino World posters Mr. Diggs left here yesterday?" Jessie asked. "I'm positive I saw them when we left."

Dr. Skyler came over to Jessie. "What are you talking about? Only my sky show programs were here when I arrived this morning. Perhaps you mislaid them when you were working here. That's just the problem with letting children do an adult's job."

The Aldens didn't know what to say. Hadn't they done a good job? Wasn't the planetarium sparkling clean now and open for business?

The children went out to the lobby and watched the planetarium line get longer.

"Why isn't she happy about all these customers?" Violet asked Henry and Jessie. "More people came here because of the news about the dinosaur bones."

Henry and Jessie looked at each other. They were thinking the same thing. Did Dr. Skyler have something to do with the missing bones?

"Let's track down Mr. Diggs," Henry said. "Maybe he came back for the posters."

The children made their way past the construction area when a workman called out: "Watch your back! Watch your back!"

The Aldens turned around. The man was pushing an oversized garbage can filled with trash.

"Wait a minute," Henry said when he saw what was inside the can. "It's a whole bunch of the Dino World posters! Hey, mister, is it okay if I take these?"

"Sure thing, fella," the man said. "It's less for me to haul out."

Henry reached in and took out a thick stack of posters. "Where did these come from?" he asked.

The man shrugged. "Beats me. I just take the stuff out, I don't look at it."

"Well, we need these," Jessie explained. She ran off to tell Mrs. Diggs they would be putting up the posters.

"Now we have a job to do," Henry said. "Let's get these up around the area. Maybe if we do that, Dr. Pettibone will change his mind about us."

The Aldens enjoyed being out and about

in the city. When people saw the children putting up the Dino World posters on bulletin boards and telephone poles and store windows around the area, all they could talk about was the disappearance of the *T rex* bones so close to the opening.

"We almost didn't need to put up these posters," Jessie said when they ran out of them a couple of hours later. "Everybody already knows about the show thanks to the news reports."

"Like grandfather always says," Violet began, "sometimes something good comes out of something bad."

The dinosaur hall was still roped off when the children returned. A guard unlocked a door to the passageway so they could take the shortcut back to the apartment. They had just gotten to the ground level when Mr. Diggs stepped off the service elevator.

"Why children!" Mr. Diggs said when he saw the Aldens. "I was going back to the apartment to get you some lunch. And tell you the good news, too."

"I like good news," Benny said.

"Well, the good news is that Titus agreed to have some of you children help him out," Mr. Diggs said. "Emma told him about how you put up the posters for his exhibit, so he changed his mind."

"Now that we know the good news, what's the news about lunch?" Benny asked.

Mr. Diggs smiled. "Well, Benny, we have some tuna sandwiches and chips and our secret brownies. In fact, I need a couple of helpers, so maybe you and Soo Lee can give me a hand. We'll send something down to Titus while he's showing the older children the ropes."

"What kind of ropes?" Soo Lee wanted to know.

Jessie laughed. "Not real ropes, Soo Lee. That's just a saying people use when they want to show somebody how to do something new." Turning to Mr. Diggs, she added: "Does that mean we should go back to the dinosaur hall now?"

"I think so, before Titus changes his mind. I've never seen him so mixed up." Mr. Diggs unlocked the elevator for the older children.

Before the doors closed, he pulled Henry aside. "Right now, Titus is a little nervous about the younger children working with the fossils. Emma and I will keep Benny and Soo Lee busy this afternoon. See you later."

"I feel bad for Benny and Soo Lee," Henry said to his sisters as the elevator went up. "They wanted to be near that dinosaur more than anybody."

"Henry, do you think there's another reason Dr. Pettibone doesn't want them around?" Violet asked.

Henry shook his head. "I don't know. Maybe he really does think they're too young."

When the elevator doors opened, the children found themselves inside a cluttered office right behind the dinosaur hall. No one was there.

"I wonder if Dr. Pettibone knew we'd be coming this early," Henry said. "Maybe we should go back out and come in through the main entrance."

Jessie noticed a light coming from under a door marked *Fossil Lab*. She knocked, but there was no answer. She turned the doorknob, and slowly pushed the door open a crack. The children saw Dr. Pettibone stuffing straw inside a wooden crate.

Jessie gave a louder knock to get his attention. Dr. Pettibone jumped back.

"It's the Aldens," Jessie announced. She didn't want to upset him by barging into the lab. "Is it okay to come in?"

Dr. Pettibone quickly covered the crate with a lid, even though there was straw sticking out all over.

"Stay out there," Dr. Pettibone called back. "I have a lot of unmarked fossils in here, and we've had enough disturbances already."

Finally Dr. Pettibone joined the children in the outside office. He quickly brushed off his white lab coat then locked the door behind him. "I wasn't expecting you until after lunch."

"We finished putting up all your posters early," Violet said. "So we came here right away. What happened to your dinosaur was so terrible."

Violet's sweet voice had an odd effect on Dr. Pettibone. For a second he looked friendly. But then he got gruff all over again.

"Now that you're here," he said, "I need you to answer the phones and sort out this paperwork that piled up while I was away."

The children tried not to look disappointed. Answering phones and sorting papers wasn't exactly what they had hoped to be doing — not when there were dinosaur bones missing!

"Of course, whatever you need," Jessie said politely.

"Good." Dr. Pettibone handed Jessie a piece of paper. "Now here, I've written down the facts about the missing bones, so you can report them to any curious callers. If anyone from the newspapers or television and radio stations call, please be sure to mention the Dino World opening next week. You can also file the papers in this folder."

Dr. Pettibone turned to Henry. "As for you, young man, you can clear some of that rubbish outside the hall. The janitor opened up an empty room just down the way. Everything can go in there."

Dr. Pettibone looked at Violet. "I understand, young lady, that you have very nice printing. Here are some blank labels for each of my new fossils and the list to copy. Can you do that while I'm working in the other room?"

"I'll write very neatly," Violet said. "If you need anything else done, just ask me. I like to draw, too. I read in a book that sometimes fossil scientists need sketches of what they find."

Dr. Pettibone took a long look at this serious girl. "The labels will be plenty. I need all my concentration when I work on my fossils. No distractions."

With that, Dr. Pettibone unlocked the fossil lab door, went in, and relocked it from the inside.

The three children set to work without another word.

CHAPTER 7

The Aldens Keep a Secret

"No, the dinosaur bones are still missing, but come to the Dino World opening next Tuesday," Jessie told a caller. She put down the phone. "Whew, that phone hasn't stopped ringing for an hour. I know it's awful about the theft, but now people are so curious about Dino World. More people than ever will come."

"I hope the police and the security guards find the bones soon," Violet said. "It would be terrible if the dinosaur wasn't all put together by next week."

Working together, the girls quickly finished filing Dr. Pettibone's bills, letters, and receipts. When they were nearly done, Violet spotted an envelope marked: "Montana Fossil Conference — travel receipts."

"I wonder if Dr. Pettibone wanted us to file these, too," Jessie said. She opened the envelope and several pieces of paper fell out.

"What's the matter, Jessie?" Violet asked.

"Look at this. It's a hotel receipt from the Hotel Warwick right here in town. And this taxi slip shows that Dr. Pettibone took a taxi ride from the hotel to here Sunday night. I thought that was when he was in Montana at the fossil conference! There's no airline ticket receipt either."

Henry and Violet rushed over to see what Jessie was reading.

"Didn't Pete say he just got back?" Henry asked in a quiet voice.

"According to this," Jessie whispered, "Dr. Pettibone stayed at the hotel for three days and checked out Sunday evening."

"What should we do with these receipts, Jessie?" Violet asked.

"Nothing," Jessie answered. "I'll just leave this envelope here. I don't want Dr. Pettibone to think we were snooping. He won't let us work here anymore if we upset him." She put the envelope back where she had found it, then knocked on the fossil lab door. "We're going to lunch, Dr. Pettibone," she called.

The door opened, and Dr. Pettibone stepped out.

"Here are your messages." Jessie handed Dr. Pettibone the list of phone calls she had answered. "And we did your filing, too."

Dr. Pettibone looked pleased when he saw how much work the Aldens had finished. When he spotted the envelope of travel receipts, he walked over, picked it up, and stuffed it into his lab coat pocket.

"Good, good," he said, smiling a little for the first time. He looked over Violet's neat list of fossil labels. "I couldn't have done this better myself. Maybe this afternoon you can help me put them on my specimens. Now off you go."

The children were nearly out the door

when Henry called out to Dr. Pettibone. "Could you use Benny and Soo Lee this afternoon, too? They're awfuly good at sorting out things. Or whatever else you need."

Dr. Pettibone's smile disappeared. "No! They're much too young. Some of these fossil bones can shatter just by being touched."

Soo Lee and Benny were eating lunch with Mr. Diggs when the older children arrived.

"What have you been up to?" Henry asked.

Benny took a big gulp of milk before he answered Henry. "We saw every kind of bug in the whole wide world."

"Even bugs from Korea," Soo Lee said proudly. "Butterflies, too."

"And what have you folks been up to?" Mr. Diggs wanted to know. "Did Dr. Pettibone teach you a lot about fossils this morning?"

Henry shook his head. "I learned a lot about how to dump things in the construction Dumpster."

Mr. Diggs looked at Jessie and Violet.

"That's too bad. I'd hoped Titus would give you something more interesting to do."

Violet shook her head. "I wrote fossil labels. Dr. Pettibone said maybe we could put my labels on some fossils this afternoon. I can't wait to see them."

Mr. Diggs looked puzzled. "You mean you didn't see any fossils in the lab?"

"Why, no, not yet," Violet answered. "We stayed in the outside office, not in the fossil lab."

Jessie broke in. "Dr. Pettibone worked in there by himself with the door locked. Violet wrote up labels, and I filed and answered the phone."

Now Mr. Diggs looked upset. "Goodness, that's not what Emma and I had in mind when we invited you for a visit. We thought you could work with some of the specimens and have some fun at the same time."

Jessie shrugged. "We did give Dr. Pettibone a hand, but it's not exactly fun yet. Not that we mind. We like helping someone important like Dr. Pettibone." Jessie stopped talking and took a deep breath. "I guess a lot of work piled up while he was in Montana at his fossil conference. Did he have a good time there?"

Mr. Diggs smiled. "I imagine he did, though there hasn't been a minute to discuss the conference with Titus what with all the excitement about the missing bones."

Benny noticed Henry, Jessie, and Violet all looking at each other in an odd way. "What's the matter, Jessie? You've got a funny look on your face."

"Nothing," Jessie said. "I guess I'll have my sandwich now."

"Me, too," Violet said quietly.

"Me, three," Henry added without looking directly at Benny or Soo Lee or Mr. Diggs.

An hour later, the older Aldens headed back to Dr. Pettibone's office.

"I couldn't bring myself to say anything about the hotel receipts we found," Jessie said. "I didn't want to make trouble for Dr. Pettibone or upset Mr. Diggs. Now I'm not sure if we did the right thing."

The children were just about to unlock the elevator doors with Mr. Diggs's key when the doors opened. Mrs. Diggs stepped out, carrying two bags of groceries.

"Hi, Mrs. Diggs," Jessie said. "We're just on our way up to see Dr. Pettibone. He said maybe this afternoon he'll let us help him label some of his fossils for the opening."

Mrs. Diggs stopped. "Well, I do hope you get a chance. Why, I was ten years old, Violet's exact age, when I started my fossil collection. My first one was a small snail shell fossil. I still have it." Mrs. Diggs suddenly got an odd expression on her face, as if she was about to say something but wasn't sure whether she should.

"Is everything okay, Mrs. Diggs?" Henry asked. "Let us give you a hand with these groceries."

Mrs. Diggs shook her head. "No. I just have some lightweight things in the bags. I was just wondering about something. I've been out in the neighborhood running a lot of errands. And do you know, I didn't see a single Dino World poster, not even on the public events bulletin board right outside the museum?"

"What?" the three Aldens said at the same time.

"We put up dozens of posters all over," Jessie explained. "On poles, on the grocery store bulletin board, in store windows — every space we could find."

"Well, I looked but didn't see a single one," Mrs. Diggs said. "It's just the oddest thing. The grocery store manager, then the woman who runs the laundromat, both told me a woman came in and said she wanted the poster as a souvenir. I didn't have time to look anyplace else since I didn't know exactly where you had put up the posters."

"That's awful," Jessie said. "Here's another strange thing. All those posters Mr. Diggs left in the planetarium for us wound up in a trash can."

"A trash can!" Mrs. Diggs cried.

"Luckily I spotted them before they went into the Dumpster," Henry explained. "Nobody seemed to know how they got mixed up in the trash."

Mrs. Diggs picked up the groceries. "Everything is so topsy-turvy, I must say. I'll be so glad when we find those bones and when Dino World finally opens. Usually the Pickering Museum is as quiet as the library."

"Whoa!" Henry suddenly cried out when he felt the elevator doors move when he was leaning against one of them. "Somebody must be getting off."

When Henry stepped away, the doors slid open. There was Dr. Pettibone, huddled over a large wooden crate. With his back to the doors, he was trying to pull the heavy crate out of the elevator with one hand while holding down the "Open" door button with the other.

"Titus!" Mrs. Diggs cried.

Dr. Pettibone turned around to face Mrs. Diggs and the Aldens. Before he could answer Mrs. Diggs, the elevator shut. The next thing everyone saw was the elevator arrow change from "Down" to "Up."

Dr. Pettibone and his crate were gone.

CHAPTER 8

Dig Those Bones

The children pressed the elevator button over and over, but nothing happened.

"Of all times for this elevator to act up," Mrs. Diggs said. "What on earth was Titus doing with that big crate anyway?"

After about five minutes, everyone gave up on the elevator.

Mrs. Diggs turned to the Aldens. "Perhaps I will have you carry these bags up after all."

The Aldens walked Mrs. Diggs down the passageway and up the back stairs.

"Thanks so much," Mrs. Diggs said as she put her groceries down on the counter. "Here, bring this lunch bag to Titus."

The children raced down the stairs and out to the street.

"I want to see what Dr. Pettibone is up to, don't you?" Henry said as he and his sisters rushed along.

"I couldn't tell if the elevator doors closed by accident or if he wanted them to close on purpose when he saw us," Jessie said.

By the time the children made their way up to Dr. Pettibone's office, they were completely out of breath. Again, they saw a light under the door of the fossil lab.

"Dr. Pettibone? Dr. Pettibone?" Violet called out. "We came back to help you."

Dr. Pettibone stepped out of the lab. He greeted the children as if he had not seen them by the elevator just minutes before. "Did you have a good lunch?"

"Yes, we did," Violet answered. She handed him a lunch bag. "Mr. and Mrs. Diggs sent you a lunch, too."

Dr. Pettibone took the bag and smiled at

the children nervously. "Well, thank you . . . uh . . . thank you very much for bringing this. Now step inside the lab here, and I'll show you how to label some of my fossils for display."

The children looked at each other, surprised to be invited right into the lab. Several workbenches were lined up in the middle of the room. On one of them were trays of small tools — picks, drills, small hammers, chisels, and magnifying glasses.

"Our dentist has some tools just like those," Violet observed.

Dr. Pettibone picked up a small drill. "That's exactly right, Violet. Watch how we use one of these."

Dr. Pettibone walked over to one of the other workbenches where several chunks of rocks were arranged. He picked up one of them and began to drill.

"Ouch!" Henry said. "I hate that noise. It reminds me of getting a cavity filled."

Dr. Pettibone laughed. "Well, this is a similar process. I'm drilling the rock away to expose something inside."

"What's in there anyway?" Violet asked.

"A dinosaur joint," Dr. Pettibone answered over the sound of the small drill. "One of my field assistants spotted part of a fossil sticking out of the ground at one of our sites out in Wisconsin a few months ago. She dug it but left plenty of rock — which we call the matrix — around it. Then she wrapped the whole thing in a plaster cast much the way you'd put a broken bone in a cast to protect it. These pieces already have the plaster removed and most of the matrix. You'll see the rest of the fossil in just a bit."

Henry and Violet were so fascinated by what Dr. Pettibone was doing, they didn't mention anything at all about seeing him in the elevator. Only Jessie couldn't stop wondering about where the big crate was. Had Dr. Pettibone brought it back to the office? While she followed what he was doing, she also glanced around the room. There was no crate to be seen.

The drilling stopped, and Dr. Pettibone held up a thick object and put it under a bright light. "There's still some rock matrix next to the bone that will have to be chipped off very carefully. The drill might damage it at this point. Only someone with steady and delicate hands can do the next step."

Henry looked at Violet, then he looked at Dr. Pettibone. "Did our grandfather or Mr. and Mrs. Diggs ever tell you that Violet plays the violin and is an artist? She has very good hands for delicate things."

"So I'm told," Dr. Pettibone said. "That's why I picked this out for her." He turned to Violet. "Would you like to begin work on this joint by chipping away some of the rock? Not all the way, mind you, but some of the outer layer."

Violet gave Dr. Pettibone her sweetest smile. "Yes, I would like to give it a try. Thank you for asking me. I'll be very, very careful."

"What can we do, Dr. Pettibone?" Henry asked. "Do you have anything heavy I can move for you? Boxes or crates or anything?"

Dr. Pettibone stared hard at Henry but didn't answer the question. Instead he said, "Come over here, and I'll show you what needs doing." Dr. Pettibone waved Jessie and Henry over to the workbench where several white blocks were lined up. "There are some other dinosaur fossils inside these blocks. Perhaps you could drill off the plaster casts and get it down to the rock matrix."

The children began their work and didn't even look up when the phone rang sometime later.

"Fine, Archie," the Aldens overheard Dr. Pettibone say. "Yes, you can bring the other children down to the lab as long as you or Emma stays here with them. They can label some of the fossils with Violet's labels. I have an appointment, so just let yourself in. I'll leave the door unlocked."

As soon as he hung up the phone, Dr. Pettibone seemed rushed again, the way he'd been in the elevator. He grabbed his coat and hat and paced up and down. As soon as he heard Mr. Diggs at the office door in back, he yelled out: "Come in, Archie. I'll talk to you later." With that, he pulled up his coat collar, pulled down his hat, and rushed past Mr. Diggs, Benny, and Soo Lee.

"Titus! Titus!" Mr. Diggs called out, but Dr. Pettibone had disappeared out the door.

"Hey, neat pieces of rock." Benny picked up some chips Violet had chiseled away. "What's inside that hunk anyway?"

"A dinosaur joint," Violet answered without looking up.

"Can we watch?" Soo Lee asked, her eyes alive with curiosity. "I want to see the rock turn into a dinosaur bone."

Mr. Diggs came over to watch Violet, too. "I knew this would be a good job for you. While you won't be able to finish such a detailed job during your short visit at the Pickering, whatever you get done will be a good start."

With Mr. Diggs supervising, the older children worked all afternoon, carefully chipping the outer layers of plaster and rock on the fossils.

"Here, Benny and Soo Lee. Help me brush some of this protective coating on some of these fossils," Mr. Diggs told the younger children. "Mind you, you'll have to wear these rubber gloves. We can't touch the fossils directly, or they'll get damaged."

Benny and Soo Lee stood on step stools so they could reach the workbench.

"This is just like painting," Benny said as he carefully brushed each fossil with a thin coating. "Hey, I just thought of something. Even if the missing dino bones show up, won't they be wrecked if someone touched them?"

Mr. Diggs looked up from what he was doing. He took off his special binocular glasses and sighed. "That's what we're all afraid of, Benny. The *Tyrannosaurus* skeleton bones are already protected with this coating, but they are still very delicate. If the person who took or disturbed the bones doesn't know how to handle them, he or she could cause a lot of damage."

Henry put down the rock chunk he had been drilling. "Do the police have any idea yet who might have taken the bones?"

Mr. Diggs sighed again. "They've talked to the whole staff, and no one saw anything that night except the shadow you mentioned. Jessie and I heard that alarm. And Jessie saw that light. But Pete says something's wrong with the system that makes it go off. So that was a dead end, too. We wonder if someone on the construction crew might have bumped into the skeleton by mistake, broken off some of it, then tried to make the accident look like a theft. There are all kinds of theories about what happened, but nothing definite."

Violet took a soft, dry brush to whisk away the rock chips. "Would any of these bones fit on the *Tyrannosaurus*?"

"I'm afraid not, Violet," Mr. Diggs said. "The *Tyrannosaurus* skeleton was found complete, with every bone in place. It was a unique find. It was going to be the main attraction of Dino World. If the actual bones don't turn up, Titus and Mrs. Diggs and I are going to have to make some plastic bone models."

Jessie put down her work glasses. "But it won't be the same, will it, Mr. Diggs?"

"No, it won't. Those bones are irreplaceable," Mr. Diggs said. "I can't imagine why anyone would take them, though in a strange way, that's my only hope. A thief who knew the value of those bones would probably be careful with them, whereas somebody who just damaged them by accident and covered them up wouldn't know how to handle them. If that's what happened, our *T rex* will never be the same again."

"Would it be okay if we help search for the bones, Mr. Diggs?" Henry asked. "We're not busy tonight. Maybe we could look around."

Mr. Diggs nodded. "It might not be a bad idea."

The phone rang just as Mr. Diggs was about to show Benny and Soo Lee how to label the fossils. He peeled off his rubber gloves and picked up the receiver. "Oh, hello, Eve. Yes, I was just working in the fossil lab with the Aldens." There was a pause at Mr. Diggs's end. The children could actually hear Dr. Skyler's loud voice coming through the phone. "There, there. Now calm down," Mr. Diggs said. "I know the work crew was supposed to finish painting the ceiling. All right, I'll send them down right away. No, don't worry, they'll be there."

Mr. Diggs hung up the phone and turned to the children. "Sorry to interrupt you children, but Eve needs a hand. It seems when the painters carried their scaffolding through the planetarium, they scraped the walls and ceiling and left nicks and scratches," Mr. Diggs explained. "The marks interfere with the sky show, and Eve is quite upset about it."

Benny said, "She was yelling at the big men just like they were babies when we came here. Dr. Skyler sure gets angry a lot."

Mr. Diggs had to laugh. "Well, Benny, she just gave me a good scolding, too. Not that I blame her. The work people are sometimes careless with their equipment. We certainly can't have scrapes and marks on the ceiling, or we'll be projecting things in the sky that aren't really there! That's what's got Eve madder than a hornet right now! I guess the best thing is to get over there right away."

"Don't worry Mr. Diggs, I can touch up the marks," Henry said. "We've painted lots of things before and made them good as new."

"Good," Mr. Diggs said. "Let's clean off these instruments and put them away."

The children took off their work glasses, peeled away their rubber gloves, and went over to the sink to wash up.

"Eeew, what's this messy bucket of white stuff?" Jessie asked when she went to turn on the hot water. "It's so heavy."

Mr. Diggs came over to see what Jessie was talking about. He stuck his finger into the bucket and swirled up something wet and sniffed it. "Goodness, it's plaster of Paris," he said.

"Plaster from Paris?" Benny asked. "It came all the way from France?"

Smiling, Mr. Diggs shook his head. Then he took a scraper and tried to scrape the white stuff away from the sides of the bucket. It was much too thick and hard to handle. He moved the bucket under the faucet and ran hot water into it. "There, that will make some of it dissolve so we can get rid of it. Was Titus showing you how to make plaster of Paris?" Mr. Diggs asked, looking very puzzled.

Violet shook her head. "He only told us it's used to protect fossils after they dig them up."

Jessie pointed to the block of plaster and rock she had been working on. "He did show us how to drill away the plaster to get to the rock but not how to make it."

Mr. Diggs scratched his head. "Plaster of Paris is something we use at the sites where we find the fossils. It beats me why Titus would have to mix up any here at the lab. And I certainly can't understand why he would leave it all sloppy like this. It's the devil to clean up once it starts to harden. I'll just let the bucket soak and talk to Titus about it later."

"I'm sorry we have to leave so soon," Violet said. "Dr. Pettibone said I could help him make fossil sketches."

The phone rang again. Dr. Skyler wanted the Aldens down at the planetarium. On the double.

CHAPTER 9

Lost in the Stars

Dr. Skyler was pacing up and down the hall outside the planetarium when the Aldens arrived. "It's about time," she said, checking her watch. "Half the museum is working on Dino World, and nobody pays any attention to my planetarium. The stars and planets are just as important as those dusty old bones!"

"Mr. Diggs said you needed some painting done," Henry said.

"Yes," Dr. Skyler snapped. "If you get started now, the ceiling will be dry by morning. I don't want to miss any more shows. Do you know that during the shows today, everyone kept asking about the scratch marks that showed through?"

The Aldens went straight to work. Violet helped Benny and Soo Lee spread drop cloths across all the planetarium seats. Dr. Skyler wrapped the star projector in plastic to protect it from paint drips. Henry and Jessie set up the ladders, stirred the paint, and prepared the brushes and rollers.

The Aldens were relieved to see Dr. Skyler leave.

"In a way I can't blame her," Henry said as he climbed the ladder. "Look at this."

Even from down below, the other children could see that the lower sections of the dome ceiling of the planetarium were scuffed and scratched, just as Dr. Skyler had said.

"We'll make it a nice smooth sky again," Jessie said.

"We'll clean up more," said Benny. He and Soo Lee went to work.

Slowly and carefully, Henry began painting over all the little marks. After his neck

and shoulders got cramped from looking up, Jessie took over the job.

Finally, two hours later, they were done.

"The dome looks completely smooth now," Violet said. "I wish we could try out the projector to see how it looks with stars on it."

"We'd better wait until tomorrow," Henry said. "Let's just clean up."

"I can't wait to take a shower and wash my face and hair," Jessie said. "I'm covered with paint speckles."

"Paint *freckles*!" Soo Lee said with a laugh.

The children neatly folded up the drop cloths, unwrapped the star projector, and rinsed out the brushes in the storage room sink. Henry and Jessie hammered down the paint can lids and wiped down the cans so there wouldn't be any paint drips.

"Benny, reach in the cabinet under the sink and hand me another packet of those paper towels," Jessie asked. "I'm down to the last sheet."

Benny scooted under the sink and stuck his head inside. But when he came out again, he wasn't holding paper towels. "Look what I found. Posters!"

"More Dino World posters!" Jessie cried. "Why are they under here? We could have used these when we were out this morning."

Benny was the first to notice something strange about the posters. "I think these *are* the posters we put up this morning. Look, there's tape attached to some of them and thumbtack marks on some of the others."

"I hate to say it because we don't know for sure," Jessie began, "but I bet Dr. Skyler was the person the shopkeeper told Mrs. Diggs about. You know, the one who said she wanted the posters for a souvenir?"

"Some souvenir," Henry said. "I bet Dr. Skyler *did* take them down. She just doesn't want people to come to Dino World and take visitors away from her planetarium."

Jessie gathered up the posters. "We'd better show these to Mr. and Mrs. Diggs right away. They need to know what Dr. Skyler has been up to."

Henry let the children out of the storage room and shut the door.

"Open the door again, Henry!" Jessie yelled. "The lights are out in the planetarium. It's dark as night out here except for the exit light. We need the light from that little window in the storage room."

Henry reopened the door, but the light from the small window didn't do much. "Can you find your way to the exit door?" Henry yelled to his sister.

"Barely," Jessie said, "but I'll try anyway." Feeling her way along the aisle seats, she followed the dim exit light to the door. She pulled, and she pushed it, but the door didn't budge. "It's locked," she shouted to the other children. She banged several times. "It's no use. It's way past closing time."

"Can we call anyone?" Violet asked.

"The phone is in Dr. Skyler's office up there." Henry pointed to the darkened office overlooking the planetarium. "But we can't get to it with the exit door locked."

Henry checked the door again. "Looks like we're stuck here. Hey, wait a minute! Maybe we can signal for help over the remote camera."

The children tried to make out where the remote camera was located. They finally spotted it on the ceiling. They jumped up and down and waved their arms. But they had no way of knowing whether the camera was working or even whether anyone was watching the screen at the other end.

"It's so dark in here, I don't think the camera has enough light to show us anyway," Jessie said.

Henry felt his way toward the storage room. "Maybe there's a flashlight in there."

It was already early evening, so even the daylight from the small storage room window had completely disappeared. Henry reached into some cabinets. Finally, he felt something. "Hey, I found a flashlight!" he called out to the other children.

With the flashlight in hand, Henry tried jiggling and banging the exit door. Soo Lee and Benny stayed next to him, afraid of the big dark room.

"I'm getting the ladder to climb up to the remote camera," Henry said. "Maybe I can find some way to make it work."

"Can we stay with you, Henry?" Violet said. "Even with the flashlight, it's still so dark in here."

With the help of the others, Henry put up the ladder and climbed up to the camera. "Rats," he said. "I bet it's connected to the electric lines that went out. All the power is off in here except for the emergency generator that runs the exit lights."

"Will we have to stay in here all night, Henry?" Soo Lee asked.

Henry climbed down the ladder. "Pretty soon someone will come for us, Soo Lee. I'm sure Dr. Skyler will be back here in no time . . . I know! Let's have a special sky show!"

The other children sat down while Henry went over to the star projector. It was mounted on a turntable that Henry could turn by hand. He aimed the flashlight through the little holes, and a handful of stars appeared in a small space on the ceiling.

"Now look just to the left Soo Lee," Henry said. "Do you know what that is?"

"The Big Dipper!" Soo Lee cried. "My father showed me."

"Good!" Henry said. "Now, who can tell me what is next to the Big Dipper? See, it's got four legs."

"It's Pegasus, the horse with wings," Violet said. Like all the Aldens, she knew the night sky very well from many summer evenings in their backyard.

Henry kept all the children busy for the next half hour, helping them find some of their favorite stars. They soon forgot they were locked in a dark room.

The next thing they knew, the lights went on in the planetarium all at once. The children were almost sorry to see the stars and the night sky disappear.

"Hey, somebody got the electricity back on," Henry said. "I bet Dr. Skyler will come back for us in just a bit."

Sure enough, the Aldens heard a key in the lock. But when the door opened, it was Pete Lawlor and Nosey standing there, not Dr. Skyler.

"Hooray!" Benny cried as the dog wagged his tail and licked Benny's face.

"How did you know we were in here?" Jessie asked Pete.

Pete pointed up to the remote camera. "I was doing some rounds. When I came back, I noticed a light blinking on my control panel at the guard desk. Sure enough, when I checked the circuit breaker box, I saw the switch in here had flipped. I put it back on. Then I rechecked my screens, and there you were!"

"Do you think you should check if something's wrong with the wiring or anything?" Henry asked. "What made the electricity go off?"

Pete shrugged his shoulders. "Beats me. The smoke detectors didn't go off, so everything seems okay."

But everything wasn't okay. Up in the office overlooking the planetarium, Eve Skyler stood in the shadows looking down at Pete, Nosey, and the Aldens. She wasn't one bit happy with what she saw.

CHAPTER 10

Give the Dog a Bone

It was the morning of the Dino World opening and Mr. Alden had returned, just as he had said he would.

The Aldens were talking so fast their grandfather could hardly keep track of their adventures.

"We saw a man go down a hole in the street. Then we got locked up in the planetarium." Benny stopped to take a breath. "But we still didn't find the bones, Grandfather."

Mrs. Diggs poured Mr. Alden more coffee. "These children have been so busy, James, they didn't get a chance to do everything they planned during their visit."

Soo Lee stood next to Mr. Alden. "We wanted to find bones, but we only saw ones that weren't lost."

Mr. Alden smiled. "Tell that to the crowd waiting outside the museum! I had a hard time getting a parking space when I arrived. Bones or no bones, Dino World is going to be a crowded place today."

The Aldens could hardly wait for their grandfather to finish his coffee.

"Maybe you children can run ahead and take one last look around just in case our missing bones turned up." Mr. Diggs suggested. "I just hope Titus had time to finish attaching the plastic model bones we had to make for opening day."

Jessie sighed. "We're sorry we didn't find the real ones, Mr. Diggs."

Mr. Diggs shook his head. "Well, even if you don't find the bones, I will speak to Eve Skyler about those posters!" Mr. Diggs scratched his head. "Lately I've been thinking this place should be called the Pickering Mystery Museum what with all these strange goings-on."

Mrs. Diggs handed Jessie some keys. "Here's an extra elevator key and one for Dr. Pettibone's office. We'll meet you in the dinosaur hall in just a bit."

In no time the children reached Dr. Pettibone's office. It was pitch-dark.

Henry turned on the lights. "Dr. Pettibone must be in the dinosaur hall getting everything ready for the opening. Let's check if he's there."

But when the children entered the big hall, they couldn't believe their eyes. Pete Lawlor was up on a ladder, and he was holding up a piece of jawbone next to *T rex*'s head!

"Pete! What are you doing here? And where did you get that bone?" Henry yelled out.

Pete cradled the jawbone like a baby and tried not to lose his balance.

"Watch out!" Jessie warned as she ran over to steady the ladder.

When Pete looked down, he saw five pairs of suspicious eyes staring up.

"It's not what you think," he began. "I found this jawbone here when I came in after my shift. It was just lying on this bed of straw." He pointed to a pile of straw on the floor. Chips of white plaster were scattered everywhere.

Hand in hand, Benny and Soo Lee raced around to the other side of the dinosaur.

"The tail is back! The tail is back!" Soo Lee called out.

The older children ran over. Soo Lee was right. Every bone on *T rex*'s tail was in perfect position.

Jessie swallowed hard before she spoke to Pete again. "Did you have anything to do with these bones, Pete?" she asked when he came down from the ladder.

Pete Lawlor looked pale and sick. "Please let me explain. I *did* come in here a few times when I wasn't supposed to, including the night you kids arrived. But I never took anything. I just liked looking at *T rex*, that's all."

Violet spoke in a gentle voice. "We know you wouldn't take anything, Pete. Did you bump into the dinosaur by accident and damage it? That could happen to anybody."

Pete shook his head. "I know I don't always watch where I'm going. That's why I keep setting off the alarms. But a couple of of times they went off when I had nothing to do with it. I just like seeing all the things in this museum. It gets so quiet at night, I like to go visit things. But I wouldn't hurt a tooth on *T rex* here. Honest."

With that, Pete gently lay the jawbone section on the straw. "When I sneaked in here this morning and saw this big bone just sitting here, I tried to reattach it before we opened. I want folks to see the real thing. But there's still a bone missing. Until it shows up, *T rex* isn't complete."

"That's okay, Pete," Henry said. "We don't really think you had anything to do with these bones. What I can't figure is . . ."

Before Henry could finish, Pete and the

Aldens heard Nosey's nails clicking across the floor.

"Here boy, here boy," Pete said when Nosey burst into the dinosaur hall whining and panting. "I sent him around to sniff things out, but all he does is keep running back to the fossil lab."

"That's what Watch does when he wants to show us something," said Benny.

"Naw," Pete said. "I already followed him upstairs. He keeps running back to the lab for no reason. There are lots of bones up there, but not the missing one."

"Sometimes missing things turn up in the most obvious places," Jessie said.

Soo Lee and Benny ran ahead and called out to the dog. "Come on, Nosey! Come on!"

Nosey zoomed right past the children and headed straight to the fossil lab. He sniffed at the door and wouldn't stop whining.

"Well, doggone," Pete said. "Not again!" He pulled Nosey by the collar.

"No, let's see what he does," Henry said.

"He'll keep sniffing, that's all," Pete said.

Just then, the elevator door opened. Mr.

and Mrs. Diggs, Mr. Alden, and Dr. Skyler stepped off the elevator.

"Why is everyone here?" Mrs. Diggs asked when she saw everyone crowded into Dr. Pettibone's office.

Before anyone else could answer, Pete spoke up. "Some of the missing bones are back — all the tailbones and most of the jawbone!"

Mr. and Mrs. Diggs ran out to check the dinosaur for themselves. When they returned, they looked shocked and relieved at the same time.

"If this isn't the most amazing thing," Mr. Diggs said. "Every single piece is back except for the hinge joint that connects the jawbone to the . . ." Mr. Diggs paused and looked annoyed. "Why does Nosey keep whining at the lab door? I guess I'd better unlock it and find out."

"What on earth happened in here?" Mrs. Diggs cried when she stepped into the lab. "It's been ransacked!"

"What does 'ransacked' mean, Violet?" Benny asked.

"It means somebody turned everything upside down and inside out," Violet answered.

Indeed, Dr. Pettibone's office was a wreck. Rock and plaster chips lay all over the work tables and on the floor.

Nosey raced over to a dark corner. Mr. Diggs turned on the lights.

"It's Mr. Bones!" Benny and Soo Lee cried at the same time.

Dr. Pettibone was hiding in the corner!

Mrs. Diggs went over to Dr. Pettibone and put her hand on his arm. "Titus, what is it? Why are you hiding here? Did someone harm you?"

Dr. Pettibone shook his head slowly, over and over. "I harmed myself, Emma. Please forgive me."

"Whatever do you mean, Titus?" Mr. Diggs asked.

Dr. Pettibone sat down on one of the work stools and began to explain. "I've ruined everything. *Everything*. I only meant to introduce *T rex* to the world, and instead I made a mess of things."

"You mean *you* stole the bones, Titus?" Mr. Diggs asked.

Dr. Pettibone nodded. "I thought people would appreciate the importance of this magnificent creature if something happened to it. Last week, I disarmed the remote camera so I wouldn't be seen. Then over several nights when I said I was in Montana, I took the bones one by one. I made plaster casts for them for safekeeping inside of one of my field crates. Last night I took the bones out of their casings and reattached them to the skeleton. But then I got confused and couldn't find the critical hinge joint to reattach the jawbone. I don't know which block of plaster I hid it in."

"What a terrible thing to do, Titus," Mrs. Diggs said. "Everyone recognized the importance of *T rex*'s discovery without all this fuss!"

Just then, Dr. Skyler spoke for the first time. "Mr. and Mrs. Diggs thought I had something to do with the missing bones, Titus," Dr. Skyler said. "I just came to apologize to you for some awful things I *did* do."

Dr. Pettibone looked more confused than ever. "What are you talking about, Eve?"

Dr. Skyler took a deep breath. "I . . . I tried to delay the opening of Dino World. I'm afraid I even involved the Aldens, sabotaging their work and locking them in the planetarium. I made so much work for them at the planetarium, I knew they wouldn't have much time to help you with your exhibit. And I . . ."

Jessie faced Dr. Skyler. "Were you the person who took down all the posters we put up? We found them hidden in the storage closet."

At first Dr. Skyler didn't answer. Then she put a hand on Jessie's shoulder. "It was me. I took down every poster I could find. Please understand. It was so hard for me to see Dino World getting all the attention. I thought my planetarium would seem very dull after everyone saw Dr. Pettibone's magnificent dinosaur and all his other fossils. I'm so sorry, particularly since you children helped me get the sky shows underway again."

Dr. Skyler turned to Mr. and Mrs. Diggs. "I've already written up a letter of resignation, Emma. Or you can fire me."

Dr. Pettibone looked up at Mr. and Mrs. Diggs. "Don't fire Eve, fire *me*. Or I'll make it easy for you and resign right now. I don't know what I was thinking. My plan didn't work in any case. Now one of the key bones I removed is actually missing."

The room was quiet. No one knew what to say. Then everyone heard some clinking. They turned to see Violet chiseling a plaster-covered chunk. Several large pieces fell cleanly away from a knobby-looking bone.

"Could this be the last missing piece, Dr. Pettibone?" Violet asked, pointing to the fossil.

Dr. Pettibone stood up. "Oh, my dear girl! You found the right bone. I got so confused last night, I couldn't remember which block of plaster I'd hidden it in."

For the first time, Dr. Pettibone looked directly at Benny and Soo Lee. "These little detectives spotted me trying to get back into the museum through the manhole that connects underground. That's why I didn't want them near me. And then Henry and Jessie and Violet saw those receipts from my stay here in town when I was supposed to be in Montana. I kept those out of habit." He shook his head.

"Were you the shadow man the first night we came?" Jessie asked.

Now Dr. Pettibone looked confused.

"I was the shadow man," Pete confessed. "I guess I should quit the museum, too. I figured out how to fix the lock in the dinosaur hall so I could visit *T rex* anytime I wanted at night. I just like being around something like that."

Mr. Diggs looked at his watch. "Whew! What a time to discover all this! We've only got about fifteen minutes before we let in everyone. Pete, you seem to know plenty about the fossils. You go help Dr. Pettibone wire those last bones to the skeleton."

"We'll have to see about getting you a job as one of our guides — that is, when you're not helping Titus and Eve," Mrs. Diggs said to Pete. "You may not be cut out to be a night watchman, but you certainly know your way around stars *and* fossils."

Dr. Pettibone looked relieved. "Does that mean I can stay on, Emma?"

Mrs. Diggs nodded. "Of course. And Eve, too. We've all been overworked lately and not ourselves. Now that Pete will be around to give you both a hand, maybe the Pickering Museum can get back to normal."

Mr. Alden laughed. "When things get normal, that means it's time for the Aldens to go home!"

Dr. Pettibone bent down to show Violet, Benny, and Soo Lee the missing hinge bone. "And thank you for helping me so much. I couldn't live without my bones."

"Neither could anybody!" Benny said.

Nosey barked, as if he understood what Benny had said.

"See?" said Benny.

Everyone laughed.

Then Dr. Pettibone cleared his throat. "Time to open the exhibit and introduce *T rex*'s bones to everyone — thanks to you Aldens!"

GERTRUDE CHANDLER WARNER discovered when she was teaching that many readers who like an exciting story could find no books that were both easy and fun to read. She decided to try to meet this need, and her first book, *The Boxcar Children*, quickly proved she had succeeded.

Miss Warner drew on her own experiences to write the mystery. As a child she spent hours watching trains go by on the tracks opposite her family home. She often dreamed about what it would be like to set up housekeeping in a caboose or freight car — the situation the Alden children find themselves in.

When Miss Warner received requests for more adventures involving Henry, Jessie, Violet, and Benny Alden, she began additional stories. In each, she chose a special setting and introduced unusual or eccentric characters who liked the unpredictable.

While the mystery element is central to each of Miss Warner's books, she never thought of them as strictly juvenile mysteries. She liked to stress the Aldens' independence and resourcefulness and their solid New England devotion to using up and making do. The Aldens go about most of their adventures with as little adult supervision as possible — something else that delights young readers.

Miss Warner lived in Putnam, Connecticut, until her death in 1979. During her lifetime, she received hundreds of letters from girls and boys telling her how much they liked her books.